083519

Thaler, Mike
    What could a hippopotamus
be?

What Could a Hippopotamus Be?

Words by **Mike Thaler**
Pictures by **Robert Grossman**

SIMON AND SCHUSTER BOOKS FOR YOUNG READERS
Published by Simon & Schuster Inc., New York

For Michael, Alexander and Leila

SIMON AND SCHUSTER
BOOKS FOR YOUNG READERS
Simon & Schuster Building, Rockefeller Center, 1230
Avenue of the Americas, New York, New York 10020.
Published 1990 by Simon and Schuster Books for
Young Readers. Text copyright © 1975 by Mike
Thaler. Illustrations copyright © 1975 by Robert
Grossman. All rights reserved including the right of
reproduction in whole or in part in any form. SIMON
AND SCHUSTER BOOKS FOR YOUNG READERS is a
trademark of Simon & Schuster Inc. Manufactured in
the United States of America.

10 9 8 7 6 5 4 3 2 1   9089819

Library of Congress Cataloging-in-Publication Data
Thaler, Mike, 1936- What could a hippopotamus
be? / by Mike Thaler ; illustrated by Robert
Grossman. p.cm. Summary: Depicts many of the
things a hippopotamus can't be—cowboy, secretary,
ballet dancer—and suggests a perfect, if temporary,
solution. [1. Hippopotamus—Fiction.   2.
Occupations—Fiction.] I. Grossman, Robert, ill.
II. Title. PZ7.T3Wh   1990   [E]—dc20   89-77080
CIP   AC
ISBN 0-671-70847-3

Can a hippopotamus

be a fireman?

No.

Can a hippopotamus be a sailor?

No.

An airplane pilot?

No.

A ballet dancer?

No.

A piano player?

No.

A cowboy?

No.

A tightrope walker?

No.

A diving champion?

No.

A bus driver?

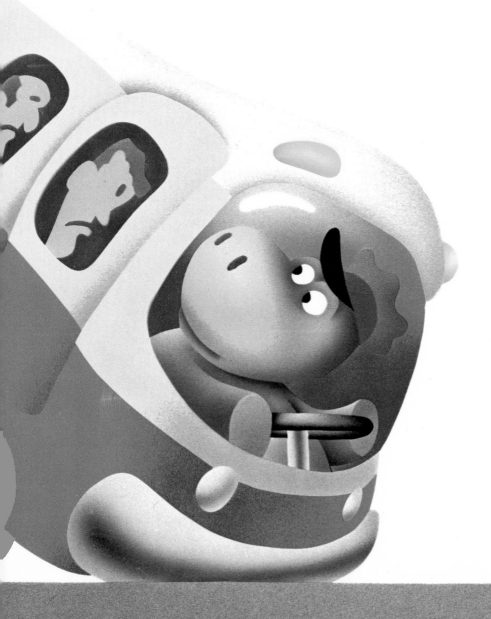

No.

A secretary?

No.

An astronaut?

No.

A tuba player in a band?

No.

A magician?

No.

So what can a hippopotamus be?

Until I think of something,

I'm just going to lie down

in this hammock...

and take it easy.